NEVER
TALK TO STRANGERS

by irma joyce   illustrated by s.d. schindler

 A Golden Book ✤ New York

Golden Books Publishing Company, Inc., New York, New York 10106

If you are hanging from a trapeze
And up sneaks a camel with bony knees,
Remember this rule, if you please—
Never talk to strangers.

If you are shopping in a store
And a spotted leopard leaps through the door,
Don't ask him what he's shopping for.
Never talk to strangers.

If the doorbell rings and standing there
Is a grouchy, grumbling grizzly bear,
Don't open the door. Mom won't care.
Never talk to strangers.

If you are waiting for a bus
And behind you stands a rhinoceros,
Though he may shove and make a fuss,
Never talk to strangers.

If you are out for a mountain climb
And a coyote asks if you know the time,
Let him wait for a clock to chime.
Never talk to strangers.

If you are mailing a letter to Aunt Lucille
And you see a car with a whale at the wheel,
Stay away from him and his automobile.
Never talk to strangers.

If you are riding your bike at noon
And you see a bee with a bass bassoon,
Don't stop to ask the name of his tune.
Never talk to strangers.

If you are swimming in a pool
And a crocodile begins to drool,
Paddle away and repeat this rule—
Never talk to strangers.

But . . . if your father introduces you
To a roly-poly kangaroo,
Say politely, "How do you do?"
Because your family knows her.

If a pal of yours you've always known
Brings around a prancing roan,
Welcome him in a friendly tone.
Because your old pal knows him.

If while eating toast and honey,
You catch a glimpse of the Easter Bunny,
Tell him a joke. He'll think it's funny.
And . . . everybody knows him.

Now I'll tell you why you've never heard
This jolly giraffe say a single word.
It's because she learned from a little bird—
Never talk to strangers!